MELODY LOCKHA

MOO

MAGIC CLUB

Maya's Hare-Raising Adventure

This edition published in 2024 by Arcturus Publishing Limited
26/27 Bickels Yard, 151–153 Bermondsey Street,
London SE1 3HA

Author: Melody Lockhart
Illustrator: Luna Valentine
Story editor: Xanna Eve Chown
Project editors: Joe Harris and Violet Peto
Designer: Rosie Bellwood
Managing designer: Georgina Wood

CH011104NT
Supplier 10, Date 1023, PI 00004292

Printed in the UK

MIX
Paper from
responsible sources
FSC® C018072

Contents

Who's who?

 SCARLETT only recently learned that she's a witch. Her familiar is Ziggy, a cute hedgehog.

 FOXGLOVE is the oldest member of the Moonlight Magic Club. Her familiar is Pirate, a talking cat.

 PANDORA is impulsive and funny. Her familiar is a fox named Roxy.

 MAYA is capable and smart, but is sometimes unsure of herself. She doesn't have a familiar. At least, not yet!

 AUNT SANDWICH is the club's adult mentor. Her real name is Sandie and her familiar is a white crow named Snowy.

Chapter 1
The Lava Sprite

Scarlett clung to Maya's back as the broomstick sped through the sky, high above Moonbeam Woods. Just ahead of them, a smoky, yellow creature with tiny wings was darting through the trees, leaving a fiery trail behind it. Scarlett could smell the trees starting to smoulder from the heat as it

passed by.

"Hold tight," called Maya. The broomstick swooped suddenly to the left as a tall pine tree burst into flame beneath it. Scarlett's magical hedgehog, Ziggy, squeaked in alarm, and hid his face in her arm.

Scarlett heard a shout, and another broomstick swooped alongside them, carrying her friends, Foxglove and Pandora. Foxglove's talking cat, Pirate, and Pandora's fox cub, Roxy, were clinging on too.

"Hey, Maya," called Pandora. "Enjoying your birthday?"

Maya nodded, laughing, and Scarlett grinned. Junior witches had to be prepared for anything, no matter what day it was. This morning, Scarlett hadn't even known lava sprites existed—but here she was, after school, chasing one. It was only a few months since she had discovered her magical powers and joined the Moonlight Magic Club, but her world had already changed completely. She had seen fantastic creatures, explored magical realms, and, of course, made some amazing new friends.

Foxglove waved at Maya to follow, then steered her broomstick higher into the air, away from the flames. "We should split up," she said. With her pointy hat, round glasses, and flowing, purple hair, she looked every bit the junior witch. She was a kind, outgoing fourteen-year-old, whose magical confidence probably came from living with Aunt Sandwich, the leader of the Moonlight

Magic Club. Foxglove was the eldest member of the group and Scarlett looked up to her immensely. Maya—who had just turned thirteen that morning—came next, followed by twelve-year-old Pandora. At ten, Scarlett was the youngest.

"You two stay here and put out the fires," said Foxglove. "Pan and I will catch the sprite and send it back to Volcanoville, where it belongs."

Scarlett shuddered at the mention of Volcanoville. Of all the magical realms she had learned about, it was the scariest. There were stories of scorching fire fountains, blazing rocks, and deadly lava lions. No thank you, Scarlett thought firmly. Cloud Candy Land or the Musical Meadows sound much more fun!

Pandora's long black-and-pink braids trailed behind her as the other broomstick raced away, leaving Scarlett and Maya circling high above the fiery trees.

"Can you remember how to conjure a raincloud?" Maya called. "It's taking a lot of concentration to keep this broomstick steady!"

"I think so," Scarlett replied. The spell had seemed simple enough when she learned it in Foxglove's backyard—but it was much harder with the wind whipping through her hair and the crackling of the fires beneath her. She tucked Ziggy safely into her pocket, then raised a hand while she spoke the words of the spell. "Earth and sky and weather vane, make a cloud to bring the rain."

There was a shiver of magic in the air, and Scarlett's fingers began to tingle, but when she looked around, there was no raincloud in sight.

"Try again," said Maya. "I'll send some of my magic to help you."

So Scarlett tried the spell again. This time, the sky darkened, and a bolt of lightning flashed overhead. A storm cloud had appeared—and it was glaring down at them with fierce, red eyes!

"That's not a raincloud," Scarlett gasped, as angry drops of rain began to splatter all around them. "It's some kind of storm monster!"

"At least it's putting out the fires?" said Maya, uncertainly.

The monster gave a thunderous growl, and swooshed toward them, spattering sheets of rain in all directions. In a matter of seconds, the girls were soaking wet.

"Let's get out of here!" yelled Scarlett.

Maya didn't need to be told twice. She turned the broomstick and headed away from Moonbeam Woods, with the storm monster following behind them.

"I'll head for Warlock Mountain," said Maya. "Perhaps we can lose it there."

The broomstick jolted, then sped on

faster than before. Far below, Moon River was a winding ribbon of silver, and the streets and houses of River City and Raintown spread out like toys. Scarlett had never flown this fast—or this far away from Moonlight Valley—before. She glanced over her shoulder, and was pleased to see that, although the monster was still chasing them, it was smaller and lighter than before.

By the time the girls reached the mountain, and landed with a thump on a patch of grass, the angry monster had disappeared. In its place was a wispy, white cloud that floated away to join the others that surrounded the mountain top.

"It must have rained itself out," Maya gasped in relief.

11

The girls climbed off the broomstick, feeling stiff and exhausted from the long ride. Scarlett took Ziggy out of her pocket and he snuffled around at her feet. She could tell that he was pleased to be on solid ground again. She always knew what he was feeling, even though he couldn't talk. Ziggy was her familiar—an animal that helps a witch with her magic—and they had a special bond.

Scarlett climbed up onto a rock to get a better view of where they were. The mountainside was covered in tiny purple flowers and rocky outcrops, and far below she could see green fields stretching away to the sea. She jumped down again and her socks squelched uncomfortably in her shoes. "Ugh," she said. "I'm wet through. I don't suppose you know a drying spell?"

"Actually, I do," said Maya. "But ... I don't think I should do it now. Not after what happened with the raincloud."

"What do you mean?" Scarlett asked.

"I think I made the cloud monster appear," said Maya, with a glum expression. "I haven't told anyone, because it's a bit hard to explain, but there's been something ... weird going on with my magic all day."

Scarlett frowned. "Maybe it's because you're excited for your birthday?"

"Maybe," Maya said. "Ever since I woke up, I've been feeling kind of ... extra magical. I really have to concentrate to keep my spells under control. You remember how fast we flew here?"

Scarlett nodded enthusiastically.

"Well, it was hard work to make sure we didn't go even faster!" Maya said.

"That's awesome," said Scarlett. She hadn't learned to fly yet, but she was eager to start.

"Maybe," said Maya again. She didn't seem so sure.

The girls rested for a while, then flew back to Moonlight Valley. They didn't talk much on the way back, because Maya needed all her energy to focus on the flying spell. She seemed relieved when they finally landed on the flat roof of the treehouse in Foxglove's backyard.

The treehouse was where the Moonlight Magic Club liked to hang out. From the outside, it looked like a small, wooden cabin standing on a platform, but an enchantment meant that it was far bigger on the inside. The cozy room was filled with comfy beanbags, and cupboards of delicious snacks, as well as everything a witch could want, from crystal balls and cauldrons to spellbooks, potions, and herbs.

Scarlett climbed down through the trapdoor in the roof to find Pandora settled in a beanbag. "Where have you two been?" she demanded. "And why are you so wet?"

Chapter 2
Flying Badges

Aunt Sandwich was sitting in her wooden wheelchair in a corner of the treehouse, studying an important-looking scroll. She was wearing a tall, pink hat and her familiar, a white crow named Snowy, was perched nearby. She raised an eyebrow to see the state that Scarlett and Maya were in, then flicked her fingers in the air, and instantly, their clothes and hair were dry again.

"Thank you," said Scarlett, gratefully. She took Ziggy out of her pocket and set him on the floor beside a bowl of magical animal cookies, while

Maya told the others what had happened.

"No way!" said Pandora, looking impressed. "You flew all the way to Warlock Mountain?"

Maya nodded, and flopped down on a beanbag.

"You deserve a reward," said Foxglove. She waved a hand in the air and conjured up a plate of strawberry cupcakes. She had recently got her instant baking badge and loved to show off her new skills.

While Scarlett and Maya munched on their cupcakes, Pandora described the spell they had used to send the fire sprite back to Volcanoville.

"It was a tricky spell, but we did it first time," she boasted.

"Yes," said Pirate, looking up from licking his fur. "And you only nearly fell off the broomstick twice."

"It wasn't my fault," said Pandora, sticking out her tongue. "It was Foxglove's flying. Things would be different if I had my flying badge."

"Ooh!" said Scarlett. "I was just thinking I want to get mine too."

"Then you should start working for them," said Aunt Sandwich, with a smile. "In fact ... there's a way all four of you can earn a new badge. This scroll is a list of all the badges a junior witch can earn. I've just been reading about one called the Junior Instructor that would be perfect for Foxglove and Maya."

"What do we have to do?" asked Foxglove.

"Teach these two to fly, of course," said

Aunt Sandwich. "But perhaps it would be best if Foxglove works with Pandora, and Scarlett with Maya."

Pandora and Maya looked a little embarrassed, and Scarlett giggled. She knew exactly why Aunt Sandwich had chosen these pairs. Despite being best friends for years, Pandora and Maya were always squabbling. "When do we start?" she asked, eagerly.

"How about right now?" suggested Aunt Sandwich.

"This. Is. Awesome!" said Pandora, jumping to her feet. "I'll get my broomstick."

"Stop," laughed Foxglove, grabbing her friend by the arm. "You don't need a broomstick for your first lesson."

"Very good, Foxglove," said Aunt Sandwich,

with an approving nod. "As you know, witches can fly on anything made of wood—from a wardrobe to a walking stick. So, it's a good idea to start with something small."

Foxglove picked up a pencil and held it between her hands. "The trick is to send the idea of flying into a wooden object," she explained. "Then you just say your own, personal flight word. Mine is ... flutteration!" As she spoke, the pencil wobbled up into the air, and hovered above her hands.

"How do you find

20

your flight word?" asked Scarlett, curiously.

"It should be a word or phrase that relates to flight," said Maya. "But you have to try a few different ones before you find the one that works for you." She picked up a wooden ruler and handed it to Scarlett. "When it's the right word, you'll just know."

Scarlett took the ruler and tried to think of a special word, but her brain refused to co-operate. "I can't think of any flying words at all," she said, eventually.

"I can!" said Pandora. "How about feather, or flutter, or falcon, or ... flapdoodle!"

"Feather, then," said Scarlett, and tried to imagine the ruler lifting into the air. She was disappointed to see that nothing happened. "What's your word, Maya?" she asked.

Maya took the ruler from Scarlett. "Levitation!" she said, in a clear voice. There was a shower of magical sparks, and the ruler flew out of her hand and went spinning across the room. It landed on the floor beside Pirate, who gave a loud yowl and jumped to safety on the wooden table in the middle of the room.

He couldn't have made a worse choice! The table made a peculiar creaking sound and started to rise into the air, closely followed by a spoon and a small chest of drawers. In a matter of moments, the treehouse was filled with wooden objects floating in mid-air. Even Aunt Sandwich's wheelchair began to rise—until she gave it a stern tap. It was clear she wasn't going to let anyone else fly her wheelchair!

"Help!" said Pirate, leaping down from the table.

"Oh my goodness," stammered Maya, staring around at the

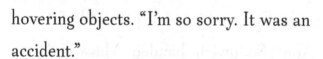

hovering objects. "I'm so sorry. It was an accident."

"No need to panic," said Aunt Sandwich, calmly. "Just imagine everything floating down to the ground gently, please."

Maya took a deep breath and all the wooden things returned to the floor with a thump. Everyone was quiet for a moment, shocked at the strength of Maya's spell.

Tear's filled Maya's eyes. "There's
something wrong
with me today,"
she sobbed.
"I've got out

of control, over the top, all over the place
magic. I hit Pirate with a ruler!"

"The ruler missed me," sniffed Pirate. "It
was the flying table ride I didn't like."

Aunt Sandwich handed Maya a large,
white handkerchief. "Surely you know that
a witch's powers always increase on their
birthday?" she said. "No? Well, it's true.
Sometimes it's a little, and sometimes it's a
lot. It looks like you've had an extra helping
this year, but there's nothing to worry about.

I'm sure you'll be fine by tomorrow."

"That's a relief," said Pandora, throwing her arms around her friend. "It's Maya's sleepover tomorrow night—and we don't want anything to ruin it."

"Of course," said Aunt Sandwich, raising an eyebrow. "The famous birthday sleepover! Well then, you girls should all go home and have an early night tonight. From what I can remember, there's not a lot of sleeping at a sleepover party!"

"We could call it a movie-and-popcorn-over party," said Pandora, giggling. "Or a stay-up-late-over party?"

"Oh dear," said Aunt Sandwich, with a smile. "I hope your poor nana knows what she's letting herself in for, Maya."

Chapter 3

Nana's Earring

The next day was Saturday. Scarlett knocked on Maya's front door bright and early, with Ziggy on her shoulder. Maya lived with her nana in a cottage near Crescent Park, and she had offered to give Scarlett a flying lesson before the party that afternoon.

Nana opened the door, and welcomed Scarlett inside with a large smile. Scarlett couldn't help noticing that she was only wearing one earring.

"Hi Scarlett," called Maya from the stairs. "You're just in time to join the hunt."

Scarlett was confused. "What hunt?" she asked.

"Nana's lost her diamond earring," said Maya. "I'm helping her look for it."

"Is it a real diamond?" Scarlett asked.

"It is," said Nana, ruefully. "But that's not the reason these earrings are so special to me. They were a gift from my mother, when I was a little girl." She took off her other earring and handed it to Maya. "Put this one somewhere safe for me, please. I clearly can't be trusted with it!"

Scarlett followed Maya into her living room. It was a bright, airy room, with large glass doors that led to the backyard. Everything was kept so neat and tidy, Scarlett was surprised that Nana ever lost anything! Even the coffee cups on the shelf were arranged in a neat line, with their handles all pointing the same way.

The girls began to search the room for the missing earring. Scarlett looked in the cabinet and under the cushions, while Maya checked the cupboard drawers and bookshelves. Even Ziggy joined in the hunt, snuffling under the rug, and squeezing behind the couch to get a better look, but it was no use.

"Well, it's not in this room," said Maya, with a sigh.

"It's not in the kitchen, either," said Nana. "I even put on a pair of rubber gloves and checked the trash in case I'd thrown it away by mistake. Oh dear! It has to be somewhere. Things can't just disappear ..."

"Unless you use a vanishing spell," giggled Scarlett, winking at Maya.

"What's that?" asked Nana. "Aren't you a little bit too old to believe in magic?"

Scarlett was surprised at how upset Nana sounded. "I was only joking," she said.

"Well, it wasn't funny," said Nana. "Magic, indeed! What nonsense."

"Sorry, Nana," said Maya, grabbing Scarlett's hand. "We'll go and look for the earring upstairs." She pulled Scarlett out into the hall. "I forgot to warn you," she whispered. "Nana hates it when people talk about magic. It's one of her pet peeves!"

Scarlett followed Maya up to her room, which was as neat as the rest of the house, with cheerful yellow curtains at the window and pale blue blankets on the bed. Scarlett knew Maya was a bit of a bookworm, but couldn't help being impressed by the number of books her friend owned. She put Ziggy down on the rug, and Maya gave him a bowl of blueberries to eat. He snuffled happily— this was the treat that he liked best of all!

"Do you know a finding spell we could use to look for the earring?" Scarlett asked.

"Sure," said Maya. "But ... I'm not sure I

want to do any magic, after yesterday."

"I bet you'll be fine today," said Scarlett. She couldn't help feeling a bit guilty about upsetting Nana and wanted to find a way to make things right. "Didn't Aunt Sandwich say it was just a birthday thing?"

"I don't know," said Maya. "My magic still feels kind of ... extra magicky." She took a deep breath. "Okay, let's try a spell and see how it goes."

So, the two girls put Nana's diamond earring on the floor between them and held hands. "Sun in the day, moon in the night," said Maya. "Things I seek will come to light."

"What happens now?" Scarlett asked. She could feel the magic crackling in the air around her and an excited shiver ran up her spine.

"A tiny light appears and leads us to the missing thing," replied Maya.

Scarlett looked around the room and was surprised to see at least twenty little points of light sparkling above her.

"Oh no," groaned Maya. "I've done it again. I've super-sized the spell!" As she spoke, the sparkling lights began to zoom around the room, leaving twinkling trails as they darted in and out of cupboards and around the bed.

Scarlett ducked as a light swooped over her head. "What's going on?" she asked, as the lights began pushing books off shelves to reveal long-lost bookmarks, and emptying drawers to reunite socks with their missing pairs.

"I think they're finding everything I've

ever lost," said Maya. "That's not what I wanted." She waved her hands in the air. "Stop!"

The glowing lights blinked twice, then faded away.

"Wow," laughed Scarlett, staring at the heaps of clothes, toys, and books that were scattered everywhere. "Now it looks like *Pandora's* room."

"That spell was meant to lead us to missing things, not throw them at us," sighed Maya. "It looks like I'm stuck with this crazy magic for life. I'll never get used to it."

"Of course you will," said Scarlett. "You're one of the best junior witches in Moonlight Valley."

"Really?" said Maya. "I can't control my

magic—and I don't even have a familiar yet. I'd say I was one of the worst."

"No way," said Scarlett, putting a comforting arm around her friend. "I bet you meet your familiar really soon. I was just lucky that Ziggy came along when he did." As she spoke, she realized that she hadn't seen the little hedgehog for a while. She looked around and saw that the bowl of blueberries was still sitting on the floor, but her familiar was nowhere to be seen. "Ziggy?" she called. "Where are you?"

A whimper came from a jumbled pile of clothes on the floor, and Scarlett ran over to uncover the frightened little animal. Ziggy had curled up into a ball to protect himself, but he uncurled when she picked him up.

"I'm so sorry," said Maya. "Is he okay?"

"He's fine," said Scarlett. "He just couldn't get out from under the clothes. It's not your fault."

"Of course it's my fault," said Maya fiercely. She looked very upset. "If a simple

finding spell made that much of a mess, just think what would happen if I cast a firelighting spell! I've got *too much* magic now. I'm a danger to everyone. I wish ... I wish someone would take it away!"

For a moment, Scarlett was sure she felt the air around them shiver. "Maya, be careful," she said, uneasily. "You know there's magic in wishes. Say you don't mean it."

"But I *do* mean it," Maya insisted. She got to her feet angrily and walked over to the window, blinking back tears.

Scarlett was shocked. She couldn't imagine wishing any of her magic away. If only she could think of something she could say to make her friend feel better.

Chapter 4
Too Much Magic!

"Never mind, dear," said Nana, when Scarlett told her they hadn't been able to find the missing earring. "Thank you for helping me look. Now, do you two want to help me put up decorations for the party?"

The girls followed her out into the backyard, which was filled with tall trees and tidy flowerbeds. A high brick wall at the end separated the yard from Crescent Park, and Scarlett could hear the sound of children playing coming from the other side. Nana had a large box filled with balloons, flags, and streamers, and the girls got to work making the yard look festive. Scarlett twined flowers around the rope swing that dangled from an old tree, while Maya laid picnic blankets on the grass.

"This is all very different from my thirteenth birthday," laughed Nana. "I remember my parents took me out to a very fancy restaurant."

"That sounds nice," said Scarlett.

"It was dreadful!" said Nana. "I was worried sick the whole time, in case I used the wrong knife or held my napkin in the wrong way. I hardly ate a thing!"

"Poor Nana," said Maya. "My party will be much more fun."

"I'm sure," said Nana, looking thoughtful. "I was wondering, Maya, do you feel any ... different now you're thirteen?"

"What do you mean?" Maya asked.

"Well ..." Nana said slowly, but she was interrupted by a flash of black and white, as a large bird swooped across the yard and landed on the rope swing. It was a magpie, with sleek, shiny feathers and an intelligent look in its eyes. There was an unusual pattern of stars on its back that Scarlett thought looked beautiful—but Nana seemed horrified. "Shoo!" she said, flapping her hands at the tree. "Get away!"

The magpie squawked and fluttered up to the tree branch above.

"You have to watch out when there's a magpie about," muttered Nana. "They're bad luck. Always looking out for something to steal."

"I think we're safe," said Maya, looking around the yard. "It's shiny things they like. Coins and keys, that sort of thing. There's nothing here they could take."

Nana gave her a strange look. "I wouldn't be so sure," she said.

"What do you mean?" asked Scarlett.

"Oh, I don't know," said Nana, sounding flustered. "I don't know why I said that. Why don't you two go and play in the park for a while? There's still plenty of time before the party."

"What if ... that magpie was my familiar?" Maya said, as the girls walked to Crescent Park.

"That would be awesome," said Scarlett.

"Yes," said Maya. "But I bet Nana's chased it away by now."

"That's okay," said Scarlett. "If she's your familiar, she won't go far. They don't give up that easily!"

Crescent Park was the perfect place for flying practice. The girls walked past the busy tennis courts and children's playground, and headed for the quieter wooded area. When she was little, Scarlett had called this part of the park "Mushroom Town" because of the pretty fungus that grew around the roots of the pine trees. The girls found a sandy clearing, and Scarlett put Ziggy down on a bench while she searched for a stick.

Maya didn't want to do any magic herself, but that wouldn't stop her teaching Scarlett. "Last night, I copied out a list of good flight words from the dictionary," she said. "I thought it would help inspire you."

Scarlett beamed. "Thank you," she said. "I knew you'd be an amazing teacher."

Holding the stick in front of her, she started to read out the words. "Aviate!" she said. "Stratosphere! Comet! Meteor!" The stick began to tremble.

"It's working," said Maya. "Try some other starry words or phrases."

Scarlett thought for a moment. "Stardust," she said. "Superstar. Shooting star ..." Slowly, the stick wobbled into the air.

"Shooting star!" she said again, excitedly, and the twig wobbled even higher.

"You've found your words," said Maya, clapping her hands. "Now, try a bigger stick."

In no time at all, Scarlett had used her flight words on several more sticks, each one bigger than the last. Then, she looked around for something else to try. "I know!" she said with a grin. She looked at the bench that Ziggy was sitting on. "Shooting star," she murmured—and the bench began to rise up into the air. The hedgehog gave a little snuffle of surprise. "Hold tight, Ziggy," said Scarlett. Concentrating hard, she moved the bench higher into the air, then spun it in a slow circle and dropped it back onto the ground.

Just in time! There was a sound of
footsteps, and Scarlett spun round to see
two old ladies strolling through the trees.

"Nice day for a walk," said one of the
ladies, with a cheery smile.

"Lovely," said Scarlett, politely, as the
ladies carried on their way.

"Did you see what I saw?" she heard

the lady mutter to her friend. "A bench for hedgehogs! What will they think of next?"

Maya and Scarlett burst into fits of giggles. When they had stopped laughing, they decided to go to Foxglove's house for the next lesson. It was time to borrow a broomstick!

Aunt Sandwich was sitting on her porch with Snowy perched on the back of her wheelchair. She shut the book she was reading and smiled at them. "Take your pick," she said, gesturing to an umbrella stand beside the door with three broomsticks in it. "Foxglove and Pandora are having a lesson too. I love how keen you all are to earn your badges. Perhaps we can take a trip to one of the magical realms soon? The Musical

Meadows are ideal for flying practice."

"Oh yes, please," said Scarlett, her eyes sparkling. The trapdoor in the treehouse had a magical dial that could transport you to any of the magical realms but, so far, she had only visited the Rainbow Realm. Many of the realms were dangerous, and all the girls had made a solemn witches' promise not to visit any of them without Aunt Sandwich.

Scarlett left Ziggy with Aunt Sandwich—who promised to make him a snack—and took a broomstick into the backyard. "We'll start off flying close to the ground," said Maya, climbing on behind her.

"Shooting star," murmured Scarlett, concentrating furiously as the broomstick lifted into the air, then jolted forward across the grass.

Keeping low to the ground, Scarlett navigated the broomstick slowly around the yard. "Just think about the direction you want to go and the broomstick will follow your thoughts," Maya said. "Look straight ahead, not down. And—watch out for that tree!"

By the time they had completed several loops of the yard, Scarlett was feeling very tired. She propped the broomstick against the fence and the girls climbed the rope ladder to the treehouse.

"Don't worry. It gets easier!" grinned

Maya, fetching them both a glass of lemonade.

"Here's to my star pupil," she added, and the girls clinked their glasses together.

"And my star teacher," giggled Scarlett. She took a sip of her drink. "I wonder how Pandora and Foxglove are doing?"

"Why not look outside?" said an amused voice. It was Pirate, strolling in through the treehouse door. Scarlett looked, and saw Pandora zooming past the window with Roxy huddled behind her.

"That's way too high for her first lesson," gasped Maya.

Foxglove must have agreed, because she swooped up behind Pandora on her own broomstick and appeared to be telling her off. The two girls swooshed back to the ground and Pirate rolled his eyes. "And that is why I'm sitting this lesson out," he said.

Maya laughed. "I may be her best friend, but I'm glad I'm not her teacher," she said.

"We'd be on our hundredth argument by now."

"Or millionth," joked Scarlett. "How long have you two been best friends, anyway?"

"Ever since we met," said Maya. "I was six, and I had just moved to Moonlight Valley to live with my nana. It was my first day at school, and I didn't know anyone. I was very shy."

"Did you know you were magical back then?" said Scarlett.

"No," laughed Maya. "I didn't even know magic was real. But Pandora could tell I was a witch, right away. She came up to me, and  started talking about magic, and …"

"She hasn't stopped since," finished Scarlett, with a grin.

"That's right," laughed Maya. "Of course,

her whole family is magical, like Foxglove's—
so she had a head start. Did you know that
Pandora's mother is friends with Aunt
Sandwich? When she heard about the
new junior witch club Aunt Sandwich was
starting, she said we should join up. That's
how the Moonlight Magic Club began!"

There was a creak from the treehouse
roof, and the trapdoor swung open. Snowy
fluttered in and settled on the table with a
loud squawk, followed by Aunt Sandwich's
flying wheelchair. She had Ziggy on her lap,
and he snuffled happily to see Scarlett again.

"Hello girls, how's the lesson going?" she
asked, landing neatly on the patterned rug.
Maya and Scarlett fell over each other trying
to explain what a great teacher and student

the other one was, until Aunt Sandwich held up her hands, laughing. "Enough," she said. "I believe you!"

"It might be easier to teach if I could do magic, though," admitted Maya.

"Whatever do you mean?" Aunt Sandwich asked.

"The extra magic I got on my birthday is still here," said Maya, pulling a face.

"Of course it is," said Aunt Sandwich, looking surprised. "When a witch's power increases, it's here to stay—but that's not a bad thing. You are a very talented witch, Maya. You should be proud that your powers are growing. You'll get the hang of your extra magic in no time."

"You don't understand," said Maya. "I lost

control! Ziggy wasn't hurt—but if I can't control my magic, anything could happen."

"I'm not sure that's true," said Aunt Sandwich, raising an eyebrow. Then, she glanced at her wrist. "Here's some news that will cheer you up. My witch-watch tells me it's nearly time for you to get a familiar."

Maya's eyes opened wide in surprise. "Really?" she said. "When?"

"I'm afraid I can't tell you that," smiled Aunt Sandwich. "However,

I *can* say that a witch always gets the familiar that she needs—one that is just right for her. We all know that familiars help boost a witch's magic if it's not strong enough. But did you know that they also calm a witch's magic when it feels out of control?"

"That's amazing," said Scarlett. She felt really pleased for Maya. She knew how much her friend had been longing for a familiar of her own. "Is there a spell we can do to find out what sort of animal it's going to be? Then we know what to look out for."

"Hmm," said Aunt Sandwich. "There are spells like that, of course, but I always think it's better to let these things happen naturally."

Chapter 5
The Sleepover

Maya's birthday party started at three o'clock. She had decided to wait until the party before opening any gifts—so Scarlett dashed home to pack an overnight bag and wrap a present. When she returned, she found her friends waiting in the backyard.

"Hi everyone," she said. "Hi, Pirate."

"Meow," said the cat, looking pointedly at Nana. Of course, he never spoke when anyone who was not magical was around.

"Goodness!" exclaimed Nana. "Who taught the cat to say 'meow' like a person?"

"Nobody," said Foxglove. "He's just a special cat. A little magical, maybe."

Maya frowned at Foxglove, but it was too late. Nana gave a loud snort. "Nonsense," she said. "There's no such thing as magic."

"Nana doesn't like it when people talk about magic," explained Maya, quickly.

"Oh, I'm sorry," said Foxglove, looking surprised. "I won't do it again."

"Thank you, dear," said Nana, looking embarrassed. "I'm probably just being silly.

I used to love talking about magic when I was a little girl ... but that was a long time ago now."

Scarlett thought it would help if she changed the subject. She took out a small box, wrapped in shiny, green paper and handed it to Maya. "Happy birthday for yesterday!" she said. "I hope you like it."

The others gathered round to watch Maya open her gift. It was a beautiful pendant in the shape of a sparkly silver moon.

"Thanks, I love it," said Maya, happily.

"Open my present next," demanded Pandora.

"No, mine!" laughed Foxglove.

Maya opened Foxglove's gift and was thrilled to see that it was an instant camera.

"I've always wanted one of these," she beamed. "Hey, Nana—smile!" She snapped a shot of her nana, and was delighted to see the photograph pop out right away.

"Dear me, is that really what I look like?" Nana said, wrinkling up her nose. "When did I get so old?"

"You look great," said Maya, snapping another picture.

Nana went into the house to prepare the

party food, and Maya began taking more photos, first of her friends, then of Roxy, Pirate, and Ziggy. "Did I tell you I'm going to meet my familiar soon?" she asked.

"Only about a thousand times," said Pandora, impatiently. "Come on, open my present now!"

Maya held up Pandora's gift and gave it a shake. "It's a book," she guessed.

"A spellbook," said Pandora smugly, watching her friend rip off the wrapping paper to reveal an ancient-looking book with a black cat on the front. "All the spells inside are about familiars. I spent weeks tracking it down!"

"Ooh," said Maya. "Is there a spell to make your familiar appear quicker?"

"Of course there is," Pandora said. "A good one, too! My cousin said that her friend's sister tried it a few years ago."

"Did it work?" asked Foxglove.

"Totally," said Pandora. "Her tortoise knocked on the front door the very next day."

"How does a tortoise knock?" asked Pirate, but Pandora ignored him.

"Let's do it now," she said. "It will be fun! I bought candles and everything."

Maya screwed up her nose. "I'm not doing any magic at the moment," she said. "Can you do the spell for me? As a birthday present?"

"Aunt Sandwich said it's better for these things to happen on their own," said Scarlett, doubtfully. "What if something goes wrong?"

"It won't," said Pandora, confidently. "Just

ask my cousin's friend's sister's tortoise!"

That settled it. Chattering enthusiastically, the girls went up to Maya's bedroom to perform the spell. Scarlett was surprised to see that everything was neat and tidy again. Maya must have worked hard to sort out the mess they had made with the finding spell.

Pandora handed out four white candles. "We all have to stand in a circle," she said. "You too, Maya! Don't worry, you don't have to do anything magical! Just make sure you blow out the candle at the right time. I'll tell you when. It's really important that everyone does it at exactly at the same time."

Foxglove carefully lit the candles, then Pandora opened the spellbook at the right page and began to read. "Dog or cat or fox or deer, let this witch's friend draw near," she said, in a low voice. Then, she paused dramatically, and stared around the room. "Ready?" she hissed, holding up her candle. "One ... two ... three ... blow!"

All the girls blew out their candles and at once there was a fluttering sound from the window.

"Oh my goodness," squeaked Maya. "It's the magpie we saw this morning. She *was* my familiar after all!"

"What are you waiting for?" squealed Pandora. "Let her in!"

Before Maya had a chance to open the window, the girls heard Nana calling up the stairs that it was time to eat.

"At last," said Pirate, bounding out from under Maya's bed. "I'm starving."

His sudden appearance seemed to scare the magpie, who gave a loud squawk and flew away from the windowsill in alarm.

"Pie!" groaned Foxglove. "You frightened her away."

"Pfff!" said Pirate, scornfully. "It takes more than that to frighten a familiar."

Scarlett crossed over to the window and saw that the magpie had perched on the tree with the rope swing again, and was regarding them with her bright, black eyes. "Do you have a name for her?" she asked.

"No, I haven't thought of anything yet," said Maya.

"Your familiar's name usually comes to you right away," said Pandora.

"How about Mag?" said Maya. "No, that's not it. Or ... Pie?"

"I don't think so," said Pirate.

Scarlett scooped up Ziggy and snuggled him close, glad that he was her familiar. There was something about the magpie that made her feel a little nervous. I'm just being silly, she told herself. If the magpie was

Maya's familiar, she would be sure to love her, just like she loved Ziggy—and Roxy and Pirate, of course.

The girls went out into the backyard, where there was pizza, salad, and homemade lemonade waiting for them. It all tasted amazing! The girls lazed about on the picnic blankets as they ate, chatting about non-magical things just in case Nana overheard. Every now and then, Maya checked the tree and was pleased to see that the magpie was still there, high in the branches. The longer the bird waited around, the more convinced she was that her familiar had finally arrived.

When they had finished eating, the girls took turns pushing each other on the rope swing. Even Roxy and Ziggy had a turn.

Pirate had disappeared under the table to eat the leftover pizza.

"Does anyone want any more food?" asked Nana.

"No, thank you," said Maya.

"I'm so full I'll never eat anything else again," added Pandora, from the rope swing.

"Not even a slice of birthday cake?" asked Nana, her eyes twinkling.

"Oh, that's different!" Pandora said, jumping down immediately. "There's always room for cake ..."

"I thought so," said Nana. "If you girls help me clear the table, I'll fetch the cake."

Nana carried the cake out into the yard, loudly singing the birthday song. The sight of it made Scarlett's mouth water! There was creamy, pink frosting, a dusting of silver sprinkles, and thirteen pink-and-white striped candles flickering on top.

Nana came to the end of the song, and was about to set the cake down on the table, when something very strange happened. A little white hare hopped out from behind a tree and looked at them, twitching her nose. She lolloped across the grass, and around the table, then tripped over a picnic blanket and went rolling into Nana—and the cake.

"My cake!" wailed Maya, as chunks of sponge and frosting went flying through the air, and splashed all over the grass.

The hare picked herself up with a little shake, then dashed off into a hedge. Pirate raced forward and began to lick pink frosting from the grass.

"Ah well," said Nana, with a rueful smile. "At least my hard work wasn't for nothing. Er ... can cats eat birthday cake?"

"Meow," said Pirate firmly, and it was clear that he meant this one certainly could.

Nana went back into the house to fetch a dustpan and brush, and the girls stared at the smushed cake.

"It's not really a birthday party without cake," said Maya, sadly.

"No problem," said Foxglove. "I can magic up some cupcakes before Nana gets back. They won't taste *quite* as good as non-magical ones, but they're good in a pinch! Chocolate or vanilla?"

"Chocolate, please," said Maya, cheering up at once.

Foxglove waved a hand in the air and four cupcakes appeared on the table. "Pink or blue icing?" she asked.

"Blue!" said Pandora.

Foxglove waved a hand and a swirl of sparkling frosting appeared on each cake.

"And finally—sprinkles or cherries on top?" Foxglove asked.

"Sprinkles, please," said Scarlett. "I'm allergic to cherries."

As soon as she said it, Maya let out a loud gasp. "Oh no!" she said. "I didn't know you were allergic to cherries."

"Er ... that's okay," said Scarlett, feeling confused. "I don't think I ever told any of you."

"But my birthday cake—the one Nana dropped—had cherries in it," said Maya, wide-eyed. "It looks like we've just had a really lucky escape!"

Chapter 6
Twitch Returns

Scarlett put her bowl of popcorn down on the floor and snuggled into her sleeping bag. There was an old movie about a friendly ghost playing on the television, but she was already starting to feel drowsy. The girls were all sleeping in Maya's living room, and had planned to stay up as late as they could,

but it had been a busy day, and Scarlett still felt tired from her flying lesson. Her eyelids had just began to droop when she heard a loud thump.

"What was that?" she said, sitting bolt upright.

Maya scrambled to her feet and turned on the light. "I think it came from the bathroom," she said.

"It's probably your nana," said Pandora, sleepily.

"No, she went upstairs to bed," said Maya.

There was a strange scuffling noise and another thump.

"Is your house haunted?" asked Scarlett, in a terrified squeak, pulling the sleeping bag up to her ears.

"What? No!" said Maya, indignantly.

"No more spooky movies for you, Scarlett," grinned Foxglove, getting to her feet. "Come on, let's investigate."

The girls tiptoed out into the dark corridor and slowly pushed open the bathroom door. There was nothing there but a trail of muddy paw prints.

"Pirate?" said Foxglove. "Was that you?"

"Excuse me?" said Pirate, with a disgruntled sniff. "Those tiny paw prints look nothing like mine."

"They're not Roxy's either," said Pandora. "And they're too big to be Ziggy's. It looks like we'll have to follow the trail."

The muddy prints led out of the bathroom

and down the hall. The girls followed them into the kitchen and there, sitting under the table, was the little white hare.

Maya bent down and held out a hand. "Hello there," she said. "What are you doing in here? Haven't you caused enough mischief for one day?"

The hare hopped forward and snuffled Maya's fingers with her twitchy nose.

"I guess she is kind of cute," said Maya. "Let's call her Twitch."

Pirate approached the hare and sniffed it carefully.

75

"I smell magic," he said. "I wouldn't be surprised if this was your familiar, Maya. Why else would she feel the need to break into your house? She's come in answer to that spell you did this afternoon."

"No, I don't think so," said Maya. "The magpie appeared *straight* after the spell, remember? And why would a familiar ruin my birthday cake? This hare's just lost."

Maya opened the kitchen door and snapped her fingers. "Out you go," she said. Outside, the night was dark and still, and Scarlett could see twinkling stars dotting the sky. Twitch cocked her head to one side, then turned and lolloped back into the hallway.

"Stop, Twitch, you're going the wrong way," groaned Maya. "And you're leaving muddy footprints all over the carpet."

But Twitch didn't stop! She skidded around the corner and leaped into the air, bashing into a vase of flowers that was standing on a chest of drawers. The delicate blue-and-white vase rocked from side to side, then fell to the floor with a loud crash.

"This has to be the clumsiest creature in the world," groaned Maya. "She can't be my familiar! Help me catch her, Pan, before she does any more damage."

Pandora fetched a blanket, and the girls bundled the hare up in it, then carefully set her free in the backyard.

77

Maya shut the door firmly behind her, then turned to see her nana coming down the stairs.

"What's going on down here?" Nana asked. "Is everyone all right? I heard a noise."

"The hare snuck into the house and knocked over your vase," Maya explained.

"Really?" said Nana. It was clear to see she didn't believe her granddaughter's explanation. Luckily, there was proof ...

"Look at the paw prints on the floor," said Pandora.

Nana looked at the muddy prints and frowned. "Well, that is very strange," she said, eventually.

78

She fetched a dustpan and brush and began to sweep up the broken pieces of vase. "Stay back, girls," she said. "Some of these bits are quite sharp." Suddenly, she stopped what she was doing and gave a small gasp. "I don't believe it!"

"What is it?" Maya asked anxiously. "Have you hurt yourself?"

"No, dear, nothing like that," said Nana. "I've found my missing earring!"

The girls crowded around to look at the sparkling diamond in Nana's hand.

"It's beautiful," said Pandora.

"No wonder we couldn't find it this morning," Nana said. "It must have fallen into the vase when I was arranging these flowers. Oh, I am so pleased to have it back."

"It's a shame the vase had to break for you to find it," said Scarlett.

"Not really," said Nana, with a wink. "To tell the truth, I never liked that vase much anyway."

The next morning, Scarlett woke up to the delicious smell of pancakes. Pandora and Foxglove were still snoring gently in their sleeping bags, but Maya was already up—and staring out of the window. "The magpie's back," she said, flapping her hands excitedly.

"Shh," mumbled Pandora. "I'm still asleep."

"Breakfast's ready," called Nana from the kitchen.

"I'm awake! I'm awake!" said Pandora, scrambling to her feet. "Nana makes the best pancakes!"

Scarlett enjoyed a tasty breakfast of home-made pancakes, with chopped banana, bacon, and maple syrup, but Maya couldn't stop squirming on her seat and urging everyone to hurry up. When they had finished eating, she danced around impatiently while everyone got dressed, then led them out into the yard.

The magpie was perched on the roof of the house. She fluttered closer and regarded the girls with interest.

"It's like Aunt Sandwich said," said Maya. "The nearer she comes, the more I feel my magic calming down."

Suddenly, there was a scuffling noise in the bushes beside the house. It was Twitch! She hopped out and collided with a ladder that was leaning against the wall. It clattered to the ground and the magpie flew away with an alarmed squawk.

"What is wrong with you, Twitch?" said Maya, staring after the beautiful bird in despair. "Go away! You keep ruining everything!"

"Poor Twitch," said Pandora, as the hare hopped sadly back into the bushes.

"Huh!" said Maya. "Trust you to be on her side."

"What's that supposed to mean?" asked Pandora, indignantly.

"Shhh, you two," said Foxglove. Then she grinned. "You know

what would cheer us up? A flying lesson ... in the woods!"

Excitedly, the girls went back into the house, the quarrel forgotten. They found Nana tidying the living room. All their overnight bags had been packed and were sitting in a line by the front door.

"Are you trying to get rid of us?" joked Pandora.

"Oh goodness, no," said Nana, blushing. "I just like to keep everything nice and tidy. When I was a little girl, I got in a lot of trouble if my room was a mess, so I learned to keep it as neat as possible. I guess it just became a habit."

The girls told Nana they were going to Moonbeam Woods to try out Maya's new camera, and she packed them a bag of snacks. "Have a lovely time," she called, waving from the window as they set off in the sunshine.

It was lovely to be out in the woods. The sunlight fell in shafts through the trees as the girls wandered along the sandy paths, chatting happily. After a while, they found a clearing and stopped to sit on a mossy log. Maya was just opening her bag to see what snacks Nana had packed, when there was a flutter in the trees, and the magpie appeared.

"She followed us!" Scarlett exclaimed.

The little bird hopped onto Maya's hand and cocked her head to one side. "I really do feel calmer when she's around," Maya said, dreamily stroking the bird's feathers. "I bet if I try a spell now, my magic will be back to normal."

Pandora handed her
a stick. "Make this fly,"
she suggested.

"Okay," said Maya.
She spoke her flight word.
"Levitation!"

Scarlett braced herself for
a sudden flurry of floating sticks but, to her
surprise, nothing happened. Even the stick
in Maya's hand didn't move. Instead, the
magpie gave a loud squawk and launched
into the air. She circled around Maya's
head three times. On the third circuit, a
shimmering, egg-shaped crystal appeared in
her beak.

Maya put a hand to her head. "I feel
dizzy," she said.

"I don't want to alarm anyone," said Pirate, "but I think that mischievous magpie has stolen Maya's magic."

"What?" said Maya. She had gone very pale. "How?"

"She's put it in that crystal egg," said Pirate, with a shrug. "If you want it back, you'll have to be quick."

The magpie soared into the air and began to flap away through the trees.

"I'll catch her," said Foxglove, quickly. Her eyes darted around the clearing until she saw a large branch lying on the ground. She jumped on and swooped up into the air after the bird.

"Wait for me," called Pandora, grabbing

86

Roxy, and hunting around for another suitable branch.

Scarlett sat on the log beside Maya and put an arm around her. Maya was clutching the camera and her hands were trembling. "Are you okay?" Scarlett asked.

"I'm not sure," said Maya, faintly. "I feel sort of ... empty. Pirate's right. My magic's all gone."

Pandora stopped looking for a branch and sat down on the log beside Maya. "I'm so sorry," she said. Roxy put her snout on Maya's lap and whined gently.

There was a whoosh of air, and Foxglove landed beside them with a thump. "It's no good," she said. "The magpie was too fast— she got away."

Chapter 7

The Magpie and Magic

Maya put her head in her hands. "The reason I felt calm when the magpie was around was because she was stealing my magic," she said, gulping back tears. "How could I have been so silly?"

"It's not your fault," said Foxglove, soothingly.

"You don't understand," wailed Maya. "I wished for my magic to go away!"

Pandora and Foxglove stared at their friend in disbelief.

"What?" Pandora screeched. "Why would you do something like that?"

Foxglove threw her a warning look.

"When did you make that wish, Maya?" she asked, gently.

"Yesterday," sniffed Maya. "I didn't mean for it all to go away—just the extra bit I got on my birthday. Now everything feels wrong. I want it back again!"

"Then we'll get it back," said Foxglove. "Somehow ..."

Scarlett felt Ziggy scrabbling to get out of her pocket. She put him down on the sandy ground and watched him scurry away into the trees. He snuffled around for a moment, as if he was seaching for something, then trotted back with one of the magpie's black-and-white feathers in his mouth.

"Ziggy, you're a genius!" Scarlett said.

89

"We can use the finding spell to track the magpie."

Pandora, Scarlett, and Foxglove sat down on the grass and held hands over the sparkling feather. Maya watched anxiously from the log, unable to join in, as Scarlett recited the words of the spell.

This time, a single, tiny white light appeared, dancing in the air above them.

"That's what should have happened yesterday," said Maya, with a sad smile. "Now, it should lead us to the magpie. Just watch where it goes."

All of a sudden, the light shot higher into the air. It spun in a circle, then dived toward the ground, disappearing in the grass. The girls stared at each other in astonishment.

"Does that mean the magpie's gone underground?" Scarlett asked.

"I guess so," said Foxglove, looking puzzled. "What's underground?"

"Worms, mostly," said Pirate. "And moles."

"Hush, Pirate, let me think," said Foxglove. She opened her eyes wide. "Maybe she's gone to the Crystal Caves!"

Scarlett stared. The Crystal Caves that lay deep below Moonlight Valley had always seemed like a myth or a legend. The caves were carved out of glittering gemstones, surrounding a mysterious lake called the Bottomless Pool. They were the reason that the town was so magical, as they were the place where the magical realms touched this world.

"I've never heard of anyone going there," said Maya, uncertainly. "The caves can only be reached by magic, and ... they're supposed to be really dangerous."

The girls walked back to Foxglove's house, deep in thought.

"Should we tell Aunt Sandwich?" Scarlett asked. "I'm sure she'll know what to do."

The others agreed, but when they reached the treehouse, they found a note pinned to the door.

GONE TO J.W.C.L.A.P.P.

BACK LATE.

AUNT S.

"What does that mean?" asked Scarlett, trying to read the strange word. "Is it code?"

"It stands for the Junior Witch Club

Leaders' Annual Potion Picnic," translated Foxglove. "Best not to bother her. I'm sure there's something in one of these old books that can help us."

"It will take months to search through them all," Pandora said, looking horrified.

"Not if we all help," said Foxglove, sternly.

"No," said Pandora. "Then, it will only take weeks ..."

There was a scuffling noise from the trapdoor, and Scarlett jumped in surprise. She looked up, wondering if the magpie had come back. Instead, she saw Twitch's white face peering back at her. The little hare tried to hop into the room, but lost her balance, and tumbled

93

down instead. She skidded across the floor, then jumped to her feet and bounced over a large pile of books, sending them flying.

"Twitch!" Maya groaned. "I might have known."

Scarlett went to make sure the little hare was unhurt, and noticed that one of the books had fallen open. "Hey," she said, taking a closer look. "Is this a picture of the Crystal Caves?"

"It is," said Foxglove, in amazement. She picked up the book and turned it over to read the title. "Secrets of The Crystal Caves by Maisie Moonlight."

"No way!" said Pandora, grabbing the book out of her friend's hands. She began to flick through the pages, and gave a shriek of excitement. "It says that we can reach the caves if we have a portal to other dimensions!"

"Do we?" said Maya.

"We do," grinned Scarlett, pointing at the trapdoor. Each of the mysterious symbols on the dial beside it could take you to a different magical realm. All you had to do was turn the arrow and open the trapdoor ... but which symbol would take them to the Crystal Caves?

"We aren't allowed to visit the magical realms," Maya reminded them.

"We don't need to," said Pandora. "The Crystal Caves aren't in a magical realm. They're in this realm, just under our feet! According to this book, all we have to do is spin the dial. As long as we open the trapdoor while the dial is still spinning, it will take us directly there."

"We've got to do it," said Foxglove. Her eyes were shining, as she began to hunt around the room. "We'll need a flashlight."

"Wait a minute," said Scarlett. She was remembering Maya's voice when her friend had wished her magic away. She had sounded so sure it was what she wanted. "Maya ... you do want to get your magic back, don't you?"

"I do," said Maya. "I really do. I hated feeling all that extra magic, but losing it feels worse. That magic was a part of me—even the crazy, out of control bit! Without it, I don't know who I am anymore."

"That's settled then," said Pandora. "We're going."

Nervously, the girls approached the trapdoor. Foxglove counted to three, then spun the dial. "Now!" she yelled.

Maya threw open the trapdoor as the arrow whizzed round. "I'll go first," she said, bravely.

The four girls climbed up the rope ladder and emerged into a huge, glittering cave. It was lit by an eerie blue light that seemed to be coming from the twisted tree roots that stuck out of the walls. Strangely shaped crystals hung down from the roof and pointed up from the floor.

It was cold and quiet in the caves. As the girls started to explore, their footsteps echoed off the smooth, hard walls and floor. The only other sound was the occasional drip of water, far off in the distance. Ziggy gave a little whimper and buried his head in Scarlett's neck. She could tell he was scared, so she gave him a little squeeze. Beside her, she saw that Pandora was holding tight to Roxy, too.

"Pff!" scoffed Pirate, padding forward. "There's nothing to be afraid of."

Suddenly, a strange, scratching sound echoed around the cave.

"Dragons!" yowled Pirate, leaping into Foxglove's arms.

As quickly as they could, the girls

scrambled to hide behind a large, spiky rock.
Scarlett could feel her heart bumping in her
chest as she peeped around the edge and saw
Twitch the hare, slipping and skidding along
the slippery floor.

"You again?" said Maya—but Scarlett
could see she was smiling.

Twitch hopped toward them, wiggling her
nose as she lolloped in and out of the rocks
that were scattered around the cave.

"She's found a rock that looks just like
a hare," Scarlett giggled. "Take a photo,
Maya."

Maya took out her
new camera. Click! The
flash illuminated the cave,
making everything sparkle.

"That's given me a great idea," she said. "I'll take photos as we explore. Then, we won't get lost."

There were two tunnels leading out of the cave. Twitch bounced over to the one on the left, and sniffed the air.

"She wants us to go that way," Maya said. "She thinks it smells more magical than the other way."

"How can you tell?" asked Scarlett.

"I don't know," said Maya, in surprise. "I just can."

Cautiously, the girls crept down the tunnel after the little hare, trying not to slip on the cold, glassy floor. At the other end, the floor dropped sharply away into a deep ravine.

The thin, crystal bridge that stretched across

the gap looked as delicate as spun sugar.

"Woah!" said Pandora, staring down into the darkness.

"We could go back and try the other tunnel?" said Foxglove, but Maya shook her head.

Foxglove crossed first, with Pirate at her heels, followed by Maya and Twitch, then Pandora and Roxy. Last of all, it was Scarlett's turn. She held tightly to the ropes, as the bridge swayed and clattered under

her feet. It was a very long way to the bottom of the ravine. She kept her eyes firmly on Ziggy as he scampered ahead of her, and it wasn't until she reached the other side that she realized she had been holding her breath the whole way!

When everyone was safely over the glittering bridge, Maya turned back and took a photo.

"Really?" said Pirate. "You think we're going to forget crossing that?"

Another set of tunnels appeared in front of them, and Maya snapped more pictures as they continued on their way. They passed by a rock shaped like an eagle, and one shaped like a rainbow, and one that she thought looked like a cupcake—but Pandora insisted it was more like an octopus.

"Stop squabbling," said Foxglove, wearily. "Can anyone else hear water? We must be getting close to the Bottomless Pool." As she spoke, the tunnel widened out into a cave so large and bright that it made their eyes hurt. In the very middle was a huge, dark lake. Tiny waves lapped softly against the crystal shore and sharp, sparkling crystal cliffs rose around it on all sides. It was breathtaking— and terrifying—all at once.

There was a sudden rush of air, and a flutter of wings, and the magpie swooped across the water. She squawked loudly as she landed on a strange, sparkling nest, high on top of a jagged rock. She peered down at them.

"We've found her," breathed Maya.

Twitch hopped over to the base of the cliff and thumped her hind legs on the floor.

"She wants us to hurry," said Maya.

It was not easy to climb the smooth, crystal cliffs, and the girls' journey became even harder when the magpie realized what they were doing. She dived down from her nest, skimming over the girls' heads and making them duck for cover. Then, with another loud squawk, she began to fly in large circles above the lake, stirring up the water with her wings. A strange wind began to whistle through the cave, and the lake started to bubble and churn as she flew. To Scarlett's horror, waves began to crash over the sides of the rock they were climbing, splashing down in the places where the girls had been standing only a moment before.

She looked ahead, and saw that Maya had

reached the top of the cliff.

"There are other crystal eggs in the nest," Maya called. "But it looks like they've been in here for a long time. Mine's the only one that's still glowing." She was about to pop the egg into her bag when the magpie swooped again. At once, Twitch leapt forward to help, tipping up the nest and sending the other eggs scattering.

There was no time to stop and gather them up again. Holding tight to her egg, Maya slid down the cliff to her friends, who were staring in dismay at the water below. The raging waves were buffeting the rocks at their feet, making it impossible to get any farther down.

"I know a spell to create calm," panted Foxglove. "But it's a tricky one. I'll need everyone's help to make it work." She waved a hand in the air, and a fluffy, pink cloud began to appear above the lake.

"What do we do?" asked Pandora.

"Just send it calm thoughts," replied Foxglove, through gritted teeth, as a wave splashed over her. Scarlett gripped tighter to the slippery rocks. Her teeth chattered as she tried to do what Foxglove asked.

"It's not working," said Foxglove. "Is everyone doing it?"

"No," wailed Maya. "I still haven't got any magic!"

Another wave smashed onto the rocks, knocking Twitch off her feet. With a loud cry, Maya reached out to catch her ... and the crystal egg slipped from her fingers, smashing to pieces on the rocks below. For a moment, she looked as if she was about to cry—then, a sudden smile lit up her face. "My magic's back!" she yelled.

"Then use it," yelled Foxglove, frantically. "Think calm thoughts—now!"

Maya waved at the cloud, and it began to dissolve. Pale pink drops splashed into the water, making it fizz, and a sweet smell of strawberries filled the air. At once, the wind stopped blowing, and the waves grew smaller. Soon the lake was still again.

Slowly and carefully, the girls made their way down to the edge of the pool and stood on the wet crystal floor. High above them, the magpie returned to her nest, and looked down with her beady eyes.

Scarlett kept Ziggy safe in her pocket as they made their way back through the tunnels. She was very pleased that they had Maya's photographs to follow. They would definitely have ended up getting lost without them! She was just starting to feel that the worst of the danger was over, when they reached the ravine.

Roxy saw what had happened first. The fox cub, who was at the front of the group, skittered to a halt with a terrified whine.

"What is it, Rox?" Pandora asked. Then, "You have got to be kidding me!"

The crystal bridge that crossed the ravine was broken in half. There was no way across.

"That's what comes from building a bridge out of crystal," said Pirate.

"What?" said Foxglove.

"Stone, brick, wood … they're classics for a reason," said the cat, with a haughty sniff.

Scarlett peered down into the glittering depths of the ravine. "The bridge didn't collapse on its own," she said. "It looks like it was smashed by some kind of rockfall."

"I bet it was something to do with the magpie's magical storm," said Maya. "At least we weren't on the bridge when it happened!"

It was an awful thought! Scarlett clutched hold of Maya's arm as the roof of the cave began to rumble, and a shower of tiny crystals came tumbling down the wall.

"We need to get out of here, before there are any more mystical rockfalls," said Foxglove. "Quick, everyone look for something wooden

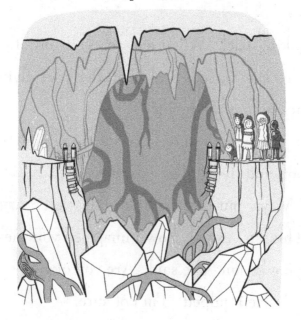

that we can use to fly over the ravine."

Scarlett spotted a tree root in the wall behind them. It was twisting out from a huge slab of crystal, and the girls had to work together to break it off.

"We'll have to fly across one at a time," said Foxglove. "I'll go first, and make sure it's safe."

Foxglove zoomed over the ravine, without

looking back. When she reached the other side, she waved, and sent the root flying back across the ravine.

"Me next!" said Pandora, grabbing the root, and flying after Foxglove.

Maya put her hand on Scarlett's arm. "This isn't exactly how I imagined your next flying lesson," she said. "Are you okay?"

Scarlett gulped. "I'm not sure."

Maya gave her a little squeeze. "You can do it," she said. "Trust me! I'm your teacher."

Pandora sent the root skimming back, and Scarlett climbed on. "Shooting star," she whispered.

"You've got this, Scarlett," said Maya.

As the ground dropped away beneath her, Scarlett was tempted to shut her eyes to blot out the dizzying drop. Instead, she remembered Maya's lessons—look ahead, not down—and kept her eyes on Pandora and Foxglove, until she saw the solid crystal ground under her feet again.

Maya tucked Twitch under one arm and was the last to fly over, but as she landed there was another ominous rumbling sound. A large crystal boulder had broken away from the cliff, and was rolling toward them.

"Run!" said Pirate. The girls didn't need telling twice! They ran as fast as they could, and didn't look back until they had reached the safety of the treehouse.

Chapter 8
The Way Back

Aunt Sandwich was waiting for them in the treehouse—and she did not look happy.

"Aunt Sandwich," stuttered Foxglove. "What are you doing here?"

"Perhaps you've forgotten that my pendant tells me when someone turns the magic dial?" Aunt Sandwich said, icily. "I think the real question is, what were *you* doing up *there*?"

"We followed a magpie to the Crystal Caves," said Scarlett, bravely.

Aunt Sandwich raised her eyebrows. "Do you mean the Wishing Bird?" she said, in disbelief. Scarlett didn't know what to say. She'd never heard of the Wishing Bird, and it was clear the other girls hadn't either.

"Very few witches have seen the Wishing Bird," said Aunt Sandwich. "She only visits witches who say they want to lose their magic. Please tell me that none of you wished your magic away?"

"I did," said Maya, in a small voice. "I'm sorry. I was scared of the new magic I got on my birthday. But ... I should have waited, and learned how to use it properly."

Aunt Sandwich's expression changed to one of real concern. "Oh, Maya," she said. "I'm sorry, too. I didn't realize how scared you were. Shall we plan some lessons to help you learn to manage your new power? You don't have to do this on your own."

Maya nodded gratefully.

"On a different note," said Aunt Sandwich, with a small smile, "aren't you going to introduce me to your new friend?"

"Who?" Maya asked. Then she remembered that she was cradling Twitch in her arms. "Oh! This is Twitch. I think she's ... my familiar."

Aunt Sandwich stroked the little creature. "I think you're right," she said with a warm smile. "This is a very magical animal. There's something lucky about her."

"I'm not sure about that," laughed Maya. "She's always bumping into things and knocking them over."

"Is she?" said Aunt Sandwich thoughtfully. "That's very interesting. Have you noticed anything good happening, as a result of her accidents?"

"Well," said Maya slowly, "I got my magic back after she smashed the egg in the Crystal Caves."

"Ooh!" added Pandora. "And when she broke Maya's vase, we found Nana's missing earring."

"She saved from me from an allergic reaction to the cherry cake," said Scarlett.

"I see," said Aunt Sandwich. "Do you feel a bond with her, Maya? She seems to feel one with you."

Maya nodded. "I do," she said. "I'm sorry I kept sending you away, Twitch. I'll never do that again."

"Hurrah for Twitch," cheered Pandora.

"I don't know about you, but I think this calls for a food celebration. Er ... do you have those snacks your nana made us, Maya?"

Maya nodded, and began to empty her bag onto the table. Four apples, four sandwiches, four cookies, and ... one blue, crystal egg.

"Oh wow," Scarlett said, in astonishment. "How did that get there?"

"It must have fallen into the bag when Twitch jumped into the nest," said Foxglove.

"Another lucky accident?" said Aunt Sandwich, thoughtfully. "I wonder whose magic is trapped in there?" She picked up the egg and fluttered her fingers above it, making the egg shimmer, as it changed from blue to white. A gentle hum filled the room, and the girls watched in awe, as a face began to appear on the side of the egg. "Does anyone know who this is?" Aunt Sandwich asked.

"It's ... my nana," said Maya, blinking in astonishment. "But it can't be!"

Scarlett could hardly believe it. "Your nana doesn't believe in magic," she said, as the image faded and the egg returned to normal. "She doesn't even like people *talking* about it."

Aunt Sandwich handed the egg back to Maya, who tucked it safely into her backpack. "I think we should all pay a visit to your nana, right now," she said.

The girls walked to Maya's house with Aunt Sandwich, chattering all the way about their adventure in the Crystal Caves. Aunt Sandwich was very proud to hear how they had all flown across the ravine. "Maya and Foxglove must have been excellent teachers, for Scarlett and Pandora to successfully complete such a risky flight," she said. "It sounds like you

have all earned your badges."

Nana was outside watering her flowers when they arrived. She was surprised to see them back so soon—especially with Aunt Sandwich too—but politely invited everyone in for a glass of lemonade.

"Mrs. Mabhena," began Aunt Sandwich.

"Call me Patience," said Nana.

"Patience," said Aunt Sandwich. "We need to talk about something that you lost."

"My earring?" asked Nana. "That funny hare found it yesterday, when she smashed my vase."

"No, not the earring," said Aunt Sandwich. "I think this is something you lost a long time ago. Perhaps, so long ago, that you don't even remember having it?"

Maya took the crystal egg from her bag. "Have you seen this before, Nana?" she asked, eagerly.

Nana stared at the glowing egg for a moment, then looked away in confusion. "I'm not sure," she said. "It looks like something I saw once, as a little girl. But I thought it was a dream."

"Tell us about the dream," said Aunt Sandwich, kindly.

"Well," said Nana. "When I was a little girl, I had a very vivid imagination. My parents were always telling me off for pretending to see things that weren't really there. You see ..." She stopped and looked embarrassed.

"Go on," said Aunt Sandwich.

"I really believed in magic," Nana said. "I

thought I could see things that other people couldn't. Then, on my thirteenth birthday, I woke up with a strange feeling. It wasn't just the world that was magical—I was magical too! Can you imagine? My parents told me to grow up and stop being so silly, of course. They seemed so disappointed in me that I ... well, I wished the magic would go away. Then, I must have fallen asleep, because I dreamed that a beautiful magpie came to see me with a crystal egg in her beak—just like that one. The funny thing is, after she had gone, the world seemed a lot less magical."

Maya rushed to her nana and gave her a huge hug. "It wasn't a dream," she said. "It was all true. You're a witch, and I am too! This crystal egg contains all your magic. The magpie took it away, but now we've got it back."

Nana took the egg and examined it. "You're ... a witch?" she said, eventually.

"We all are," said Foxglove proudly, "and Pirate's a talking cat. Say something, Pirate!"

"Like what?" grumbled the cat. "I need time to prepare."

Nana looked confused. "I think you're all playing a trick on me," she said.

124

"I'm afraid Patience won't be able to understand magic until her magic is returned to her," Aunt Sandwich said, gently.

"Why is everyone talking about magic?" Nana asked.

Aunt Sandwich put her hand on the old lady's arm. "Would you like to see magic again, Patience?" she asked. "It's your choice. If not, I can take this egg back to the Crystal Caves, and things will carry on as they were before."

"I suppose I've always hoped that I'd be able to see magic again one day, like I could when I was a little girl," Nana said.

"Then smash the egg!" said Pandora, hopping impatiently from foot to foot.

"Oh, but that seems a shame," Nana said.

"It's so pretty ..."

"Please, Nana," said Maya. "It's amazing being a witch. I've made so many good friends, and done so many wonderful things—and all the time, I've wished I could share them with you."

"Well, that settles it," said Nana, with a smile. And she threw the crystal egg onto the floor—where it shattered.

Maya stared at her nana's face. "Do you feel different?" she asked, anxiously.

"I think I do," said Nana. She patted her face with her fingertips. "I feel sort of sparkly. I haven't felt this way since ... well ... my thirteenth birthday." She waved her hands in the air and a dusting of magical stars appeared.

"You did a spell!" cheered Maya.

"Do another one!" said Pandora.

"Oh my," said Nana, staring at her fingers.

"Slow down, girls," laughed Aunt Sandwich. "Why don't you all go and play for a bit, while Patience and I have a proper talk? She's bound to have a lot of questions."

So the girls went out into the yard, and left the grown-ups to talk. Maya was so pleased, she couldn't stop grinning. "This is the best birthday present ever," she said.

That night, the girls assembled for a very special badge ceremony—and Maya's nana came along to watch.

"This is all going to take a bit of getting used to," Nana laughed, as Maya explained (for the third time) that the treehouse was bigger on the inside than the outside.

"Are you glad you got your magic back?" Scarlett asked.

"Oh yes," beamed Nana. "But the best thing of all is knowing what an amazing time Maya is having. I had such a lonely experience of magic as a child—it's wonderful to see how different things are for her."

"We're all having an amazing time," said Scarlett, happily. "And it's all thanks to the Moonlight Magic Club!"